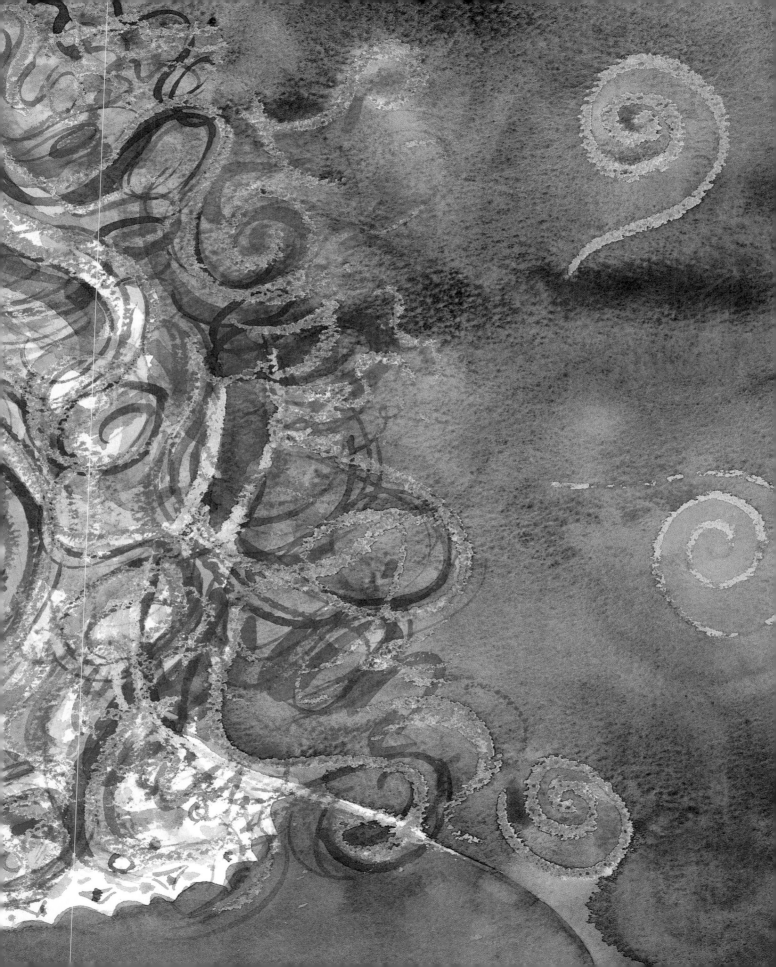

For Clare and Shauna, Mark and Laura
- D.C.

For Rachael
- B.O'D.

For Niamh
- B.E.

Discovery Publications, Brookfield Business Centre,
333 Crumlin Road, Belfast BT14 7EA
Telephone: 028 9049 2410
Email address: declan.carville@ntlworld.com

First published by Discovery Publications, 2000
This edition, 2002

Text © 2000 Declan Carville

Book Design © 2000 Bernard O'Donnell

Illustrations © 2000 Brendan Ellis

A CIP catalogue record of this book is available from the British Library.

Printed in Belgium by Proost NV. Turnhout.

ISBN 0-9538222-1-4

2 3 4 5 6 7 8 9 10

Valentine O'Byrne
Irish Dancer

Declan Carville
illustrated by Brendan Ellis
book design by Bernard O' Donnell

Valentine had a dream.
She wanted to be a dancer.
But not just any kind of dancer.

Valentine wanted to be an Irish dancer.

She practised all the time. Everywhere.
In the kitchen.

In her bedroom.

In the bathroom.

In the supermarket.

Even at the bus stop.

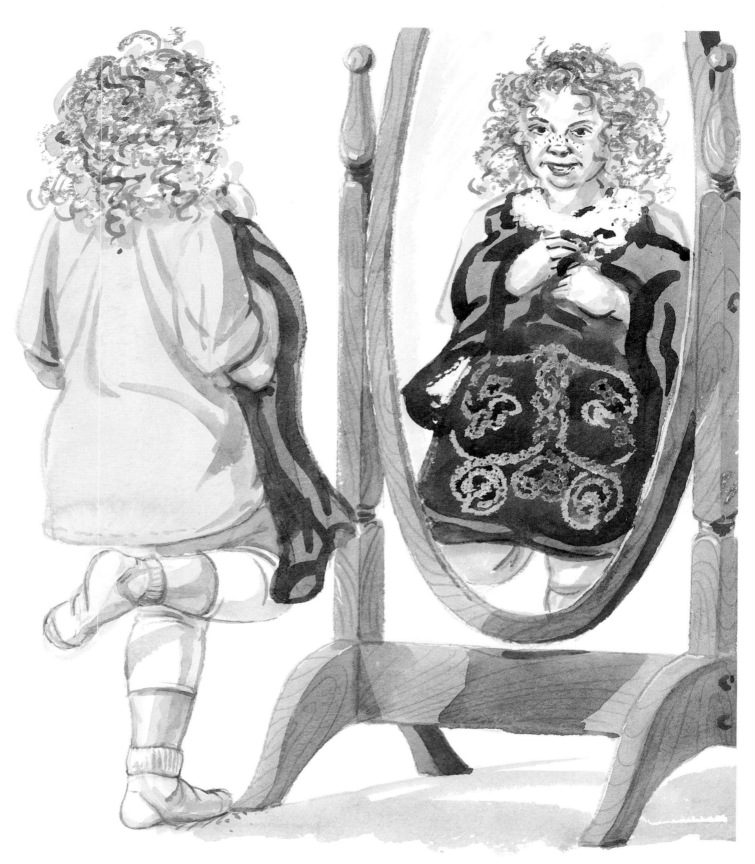

She was especially proud of her dancing outfit.
She kept it for special occasions.

So when the lady came to school
to pick dancers, Valentine was
really excited. She performed with
the other girls. She kicked her
legs as high as she could.
She just kept dancing
and dancing and dancing!
She thought she was
floating on air!

But the lady didn't pick Valentine.
In fact, she hardly even noticed her.

Valentine was very disappointed.
That day she walked home from school.
No twirls or spins. She was very sad.

Mum told her not
to be too unhappy
and made her
a sandwich.
"Go in and sit
down, love"
she said.
"Your legs
must be tired.
I'll put on your video."

Valentine sank into the chair. She didn't feel hungry.
All she wanted to do was dance.
"Why couldn't I have been picked," she said to herself.
Then suddenly she caught sight of the dancers on the TV.
And she had an idea. She sat up so quickly
her drink nearly went over the floor.
"Where are you going, Valentine?"
her Mum shouted as she ran
out the door.
"Valentine!"

Valentine ran into the house next door. "Is Conor here?"
she asked Mrs Walsh. "I need to see him!"

That night Valentine and several of her friends stayed in her garage for hours, until it was time to come in for bed. "We must meet again tomorrow," Valentine said to her friends. "We have lots more to do."

Nobody knew what they were up to. Not until Friday when Conor Walsh put a big poster outside Valentine's garden wall.

COME TO THE SHOW!
SATURDAY AT ONE O'CLOCK.
DANCING, SINGING
AND LOTS MORE!
EVERYONE WELCOME!

Valentine could see from her bedroom window that lots of people were stopping and staring. She started to get very excited. In fact, the night before, she could hardly sleep.

The next day everybody had a job to do. Mary handed a ticket to everyone coming in, so as they could get into the back garden.

Sean Hughes was practising
his magic tricks

and the twins Angela and Clare sang some lovely songs.

Valentine came on at the end. But she didn't just walk on—she ran on, legs flying through the air!

Everybody screamed and clapped. Some people even stood up!

Valentine danced until she could no longer feel her feet. She wanted to go on forever. She took many bows in front of the audience.

People were shouting for more. But Valentine just smiled and waved and said she would see them all again soon. Next time.

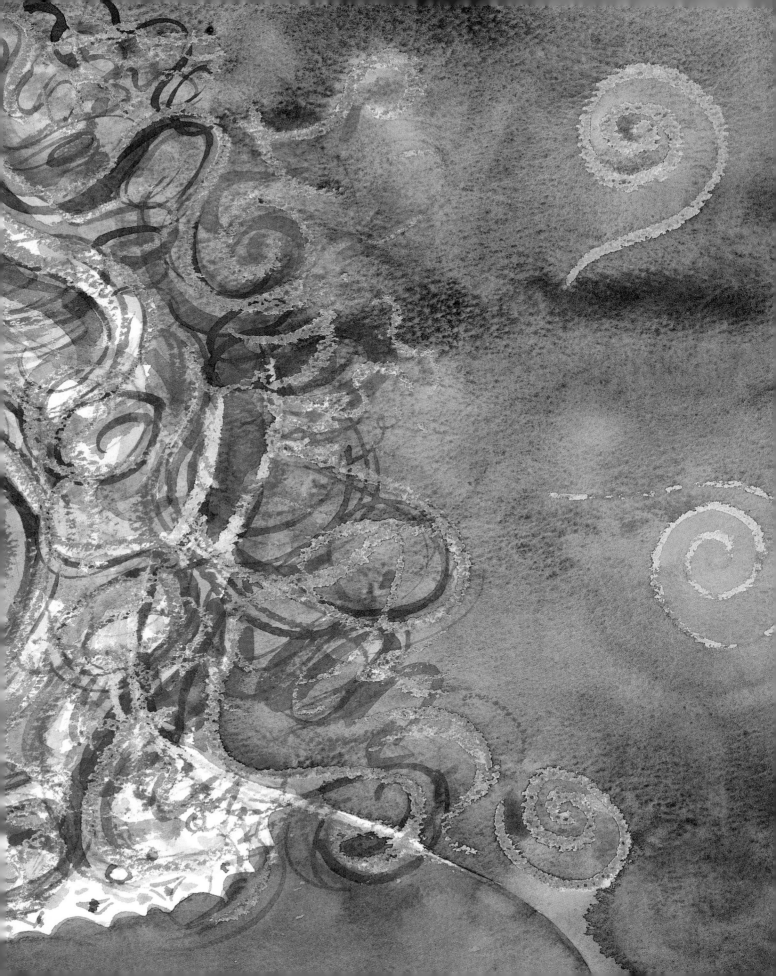